For Sue and Paul
A.H.B.

For Jess
T.W.

LITTLE TIGER PRESS
An imprint of Magi Publications, London SW6 6AW
www.littletigerpress.com

First published in Great Britain 1998
This edition published 2003

Printed in Dubai
1 85430 927 7

1 3 5 7 9 10 8 6 4 2

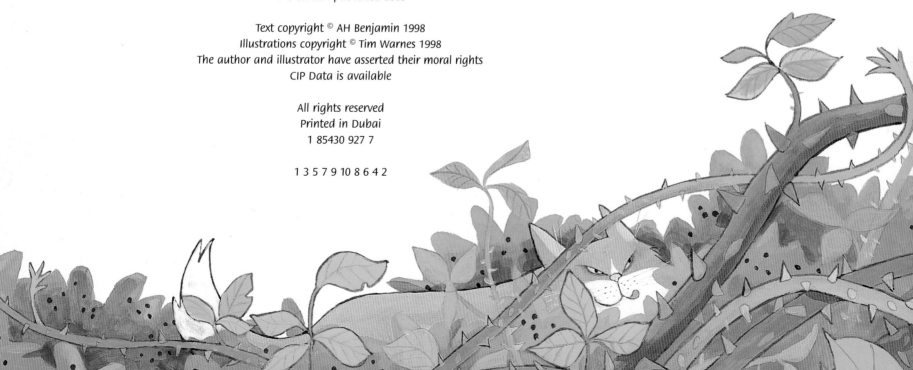

IT COULD HAVE BEEN WORSE

by **A.H.Benjamin** & Pictures by **Tim Warnes**

Mouse was on his way back home
after visiting his town cousin, when . . .

WHOOPS!

He lost his balance and fell to the ground.

"Ouch!" said Mouse.
"This isn't my
lucky day."

But it could have
been worse!

Mouse picked himself up
and continued on his way.
He came to an open field
and was scurrying across it
when . . .

CRASH!

He fell into a dark hole.

"Why do things *always* go wrong for me?" grumbled Mouse.

But it could have been worse!

Mouse climbed out of the hole and
was off again, but soon he got sleepy.

"I think I'll take a rest," Mouse said. He
had just found a comfortable spot, when . . .

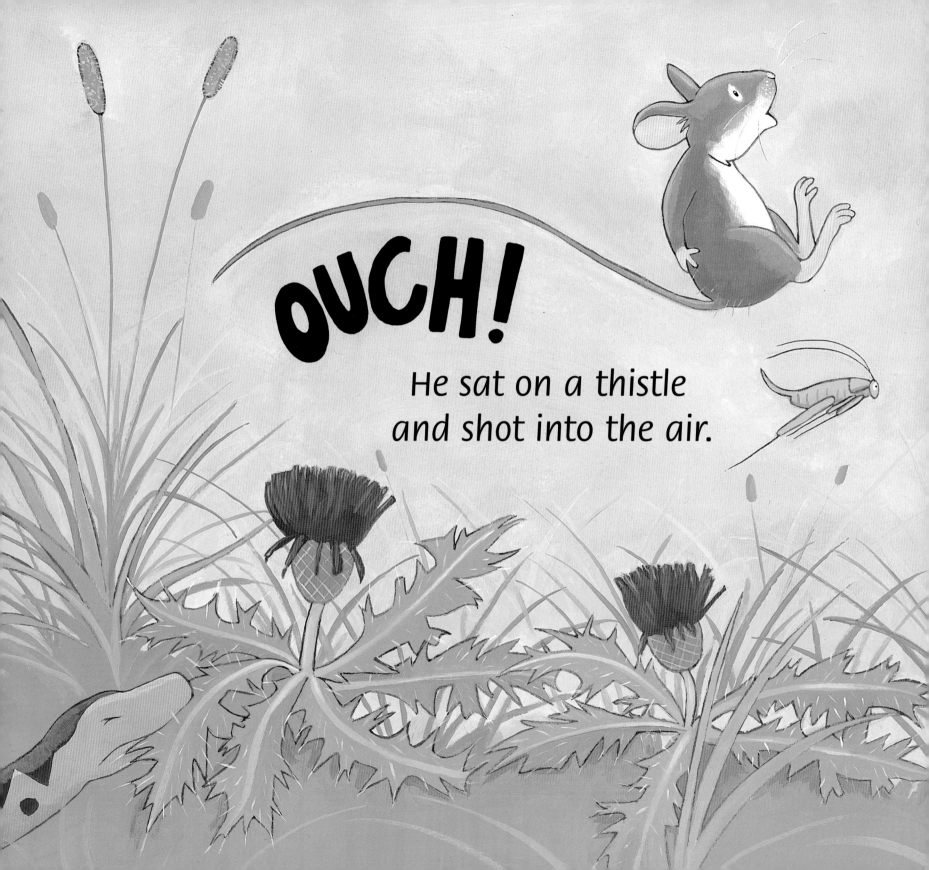

OUCH!

He sat on a thistle
and shot into the air.

"Everything bad happens to me!" wailed Mouse as he pulled the thorns out of his fur.

But it could have been worse!

Mouse trotted down the hill until he reached a stream. He began to cross it using the stepping stones when . . .

"I'll catch a cold!"
complained Mouse.

But it could have been worse!

Mouse paddled to the edge of the
stream and climbed out of the water.

Shaking himself dry, he was just about to scramble down a steep bank, when . . .

WHEEE!

He lost his footing and
skidded to the bottom.

"I'll be black and blue all over," cried Mouse.

But it could have been worse!

Mouse staggered to his feet and
ran the rest of the way home.

"It's been a terrible day," he said to his
mother as she bathed his cuts and bruises.
"I fell into a hole, got wet in the river, and—"
"Never mind, son," she said . . .